For Mike and Tysun

VIKING
Published by the Penguin Group
Penguin Books USA Inc., 375 Hudson Street, New York, New York 10014, U.S.A.
Penguin Books Australia Ltd, Ringwood, Victoria, Australia
Penguin Books Canada Ltd, 10 Alcorn Avenue, Toronto, Ontario, Canada M4V 3B2
Penguin Books (N.Z.) Ltd, 182-190 Wairau Road, Auckland 10, New Zealand

Penguin Books Ltd, Registered Offices: Harmondsworth, Middlesex, England

First published in Great Britain by ABC, All Books for Children, a division of The All Children's Company Ltd., 1992
First American edition published by Viking, a division of Penguin Books USA Inc., 1993
1 3 5 7 9 10 8 6 4 2
Copyright © Alex Ayliffe, 1992
All rights reserved

Library of Congress Catalog Card Number: 92-16415
(CIP data available)
ISBN 0-670-84801-8
Printed in Hong Kong

slither, swoop, swing

ALEX AYLIFFE

Viking

swing

waddle

pounce

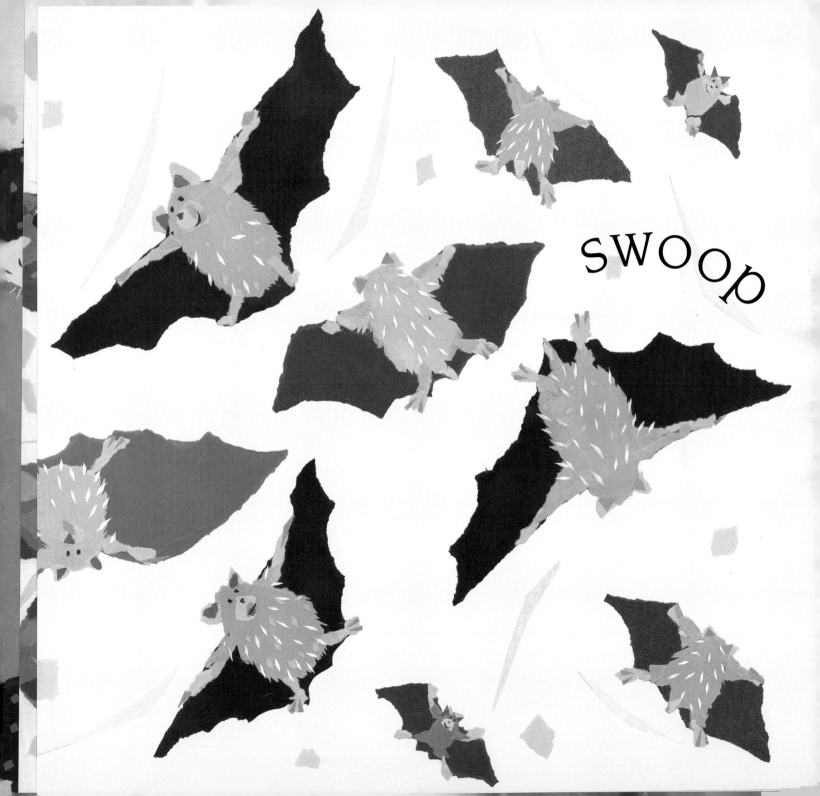

SWOOP

cling

flap

hop

dive

run